Stories of Mr. Keuner

Stories of Mr. Keuner

Bertolt Brecht

Translated from the German
and with an afterword
by Martin Chalmers

City Lights Books
San Francisco

First City Lights edition, 2001
First published in German in 1965 under the title *Geschichten vom Herrn Keuner* by Suhrkamp Verlag, Frankfurt am Main
Original text © 1965 by Stefan S. Brecht
Translation © 2001 by Stefan S. Brecht
Cover photo of Bertolt Brecht (c. 1952) by Gerda Goedhart
© 2001 by Suhrkamp Verlag
Published by arrangement with Stefan S. Brecht and Suhrkamp Verlag
Afterword © 2001 by Martin Chalmers

Cover design: Stefan Gutermuth
Book design and typography: Small World Productions
Editor: James Brook

Library of Congress Cataloging-in-Publication Data
Brecht, Bertolt, 1898-1956
    [Geschichten vom Herrn Keuner. English]
Stories of Mr. Keuner / by Bertolt Brecht; translated by Martin Chalmers
       p. cm.
    ISBN 0-87286-383-2
    I. Chalmers, Martin. II. Title.
    PT2603. R397 G4513 2001
    833'.912—dc21

                             00-065637

CITY LIGHTS BOOKS are edited by Lawrence Ferlinghetti and Nancy J. Peters and published at the City Lights Bookstore, 261 Columbus Avenue, San Francisco, CA 94133. Visit us on the Web at www.citylights.com.

Contents

What's wise about the wise man is his stance

A philosophy professor came to see Mr. K. and told him about his wisdom. After a while Mr. K. said to him: "You sit uncomfortably, you talk uncomfortably, you think uncomfortably." The philosophy professor became angry and said: "I didn't want to hear anything about myself but about the substance of what I was talking about." "It has no substance," said Mr. K. "I see you walking clumsily and, as far as I can see, you're not getting anywhere. You talk obscurely, and you create no light with your talking. Seeing your stance, I'm not interested in what you're getting at."

Organization

Mr. K. once said: "The thinking man does not use one light too many, one piece of bread too many, one idea too many."

Measures against power

As Mr. Keuner, the thinking man, was speaking out against Power in front of a large audience in a hall, he noticed the people in front of him shrinking back and leaving. He looked round and saw standing behind him—Power.

"What were you saying?" Power asked him.

"I was speaking out in favor of Power," replied Mr. Keuner.

After Mr. Keuner had left the hall, his students inquired about his backbone. Mr. Keuner replied: "I don't have a backbone to be broken. I'm the one who has to live longer than Power."

And Mr. Keuner told the following story:

One day, during the period of illegality, an agent entered the apartment of Mr. Eggers, a man who had learned to say no. The agent showed a document, which was made out in the name of those who ruled the city, and which stated that any apartment in which he set foot belonged to him; likewise, any food that he demanded belonged to him; likewise, any man whom he saw, had to serve him.

The agent sat down in a chair, demanded food, washed, lay down in bed, and, before he fell asleep, asked, with his face to the wall: "Will you be my servant?"

Mr. Eggers covered the agent with a blanket, drove away the flies, watched over his sleep, and, as he had done on this day, obeyed him for seven years. But whatever he did for him, one thing Mr. Eggers was very careful not to do: that was, to say a single word. Now, when the seven years had passed and the agent had grown fat from all the eating, sleeping, and giving orders, he died. Then Mr. Eggers wrapped him in the ruined blanket, dragged him out of the house, washed the bed, whitewashed the walls, drew a deep breath and replied: "No."

Of the bearers of knowledge

"He who bears knowledge must not fight, nor tell the truth, nor do a service, nor not eat, nor refuse honors, nor be conspicuous. He who bears knowledge has only one virtue: that he bears knowledge," said Mr. Keuner.

Serving a purpose

Mr. K. put the following questions:

"Every morning my neighbor plays music on a gramophone. Why does he play music? Because he's doing exercises, I've heard. Why is he doing exercises? Because he needs to be strong, I've heard. Why does he need to be strong? He says it's because he must defeat his enemies in the city. Why must he defeat enemies? Because he wants to eat, I've heard." After Mr. K. had heard that his neighbor played music in order to do exercises, did exercises in order to be strong, wanted to be strong in order to kill his enemies, killed his enemies in order to eat, he put his question: "Why does he eat?"

Hardships of the best

"What are you working on?" Mr. K. was asked. Mr. K. replied: "I'm having a hard time, I'm preparing my next mistake."

Not bribing is an art

Mr. K. recommended a man to a businessman, because of his unbribability. After two weeks the businessman came back to Mr. K. and asked him: "What did you mean by unbribability?" Mr. K. said: "If I say the man you hire is unbribable, I mean by that, you can't bribe him." "Well," said the businessman gloomily, "I have reason to fear that your man even lets himself be bribed by my enemies." "I don't know anything about that," said Mr. K. without any interest. "But," exclaimed the businessman indignantly, "he always agrees with me, so he also lets himself be bribed by me!" Mr. K. smiled conceitedly. "He doesn't let me bribe him," he said.

Love of fatherland,
the hatred of fatherlands

Mr. K. did not think it necessary to live in any particular country. He said: "I can go hungry anywhere." One day, however, he was walking through a city that was occupied by the enemy of the country in which he was living. An officer of this enemy came toward him and forced him to step down from the pavement. Mr. K. stepped down and realized that he felt outraged at this man, and not only at this man, but especially at the country to which the man belonged, that is, he wanted it to be wiped from the face of the earth. "What made me," asked Mr. K., "become a nationalist for this one minute? It was because I encountered a nationalist. But that is precisely why this stupidity has to be rooted out, because it makes whoever encounters it stupid."

The bad is not cheap, either

Mr. Keuner came by his ideas on the distribution of poverty while reflecting on mankind. One day, looking around his apartment, he decided he wanted different furniture—cheaper, shabbier, not so well made. He immediately went to a joiner and asked him to scrape the varnish from his furniture. But when the varnish had been scraped off, the furniture did not look shabby, but merely ruined. Nevertheless, the joiner's bill had to be paid, and Mr. Keuner also had to throw away his pieces of furniture and buy new ones—shabby, cheap, not so well made—because he wanted them so badly. Some people who heard about this laughed at Mr. Keuner, since his shabby furniture had turned out more expensive than the varnished kind. But Mr. Keuner said: "Poverty does not mean saving, but spending. I know you: your poverty does not suit your ideas. But wealth does not suit my ideas."

Going hungry

When asked about a fatherland, Mr. K. had given the answer: "I can go hungry anywhere." Then a careful listener asked him why he said was going hungry, when in reality he had enough to eat. Mr. K. excused himself by saying: "Probably I meant to say that I can live anywhere, if I want to live, where there is hunger. I admit that there is a big difference, whether I myself am going hungry or whether I am living where hunger is the rule. But in my defense, may I be allowed to say that to me living where hunger is the rule, while not as bad as going hungry, is at least very bad. It would, of course, not be very important to others if I were going hungry, but it is important that I am against hunger being the rule."

Advice, when advice is not heeded

Mr. K. recommended that, if possible, every piece of friendly advice should be accompanied by a further piece of advice, in case the advice is not heeded. When, for example, he had counseled someone who was in a difficult situation to take a particular course of action, which harmed as few others as possible, he also outlined another course of action, not so harmless but still not the most ruthless. "Someone who is not capable of doing everything," he said, "should not be let off with something minor."

Originality

"Nowadays," complained Mr. K., "there are innumerable people who boast in public that they are able to write great books all by themselves, and this meets with general approval. When he was already in the prime of life the Chinese philosopher Chuang-tzu composed a book of one hundred thousand words, nine-tenths of which consisted of quotations. Such books can no longer be written here and now, because the wit is lacking. As a result, ideas are only produced in one's own workshop, and anyone who does not manage enough of them thinks himself lazy. Admittedly, there is then not a single idea that could be adopted or a single formulation of an idea that could be quoted. How little all of them need for their activity! A pen and some paper are the only things they are able to show! And without any help, with only the scant material that anyone can carry in his hands, they erect their cottages! The largest buildings they know are those a single man is capable of constructing!"

The question of
whether there is a God

A man asked Mr. K. whether there is a God. Mr. K. said: "I advise you to consider whether, depending on the answer, your behavior would change. If it would not change, then we can drop the question. If it would change, then I can at least be of help to the extent that I can say, you have already decided: you need a God."

The right to weakness

Mr. K. helped someone out on a difficult matter. Subsequently, the latter gave Mr. K. no thanks of any kind.

Mr. K. then astonished his friends by complaining loudly about the ingratitude of the person concerned. They thought Mr. K.'s behavior ill-mannered and even said: "Didn't you know that one should not do anything for the sake of gratitude, because man is too weak to be grateful?" "And I," asked Mr. K., "am I not human? Why should I not be so weak as to insist on gratitude? People always think they are admitting their own stupidity if they admit that something mean was done to them. Why should that be so?"

The helpless boy

Mr. K. talked about the bad habit of silently allowing an injustice suffered to eat at one, and told the following story: "A boy was crying to himself and a passerby asked what was wrong. 'I had saved two dimes for the movies,' said the boy, 'when a big lad came and grabbed one from me,' and he pointed at a lad who could be seen some distance away. 'Did you not shout for help?' asked the man. 'I did,' said the boy and sobbed a little more loudly. 'And didn't anyone hear you?' the man went on, stroking him fondly. 'No,' sobbed the boy and looked at the man with new hope. Because he was smiling. 'Then give me that one as well,' said the man and took the second dime out of the boy's hand and walked away unconcerned.

Mr. K. and nature

Asked about his relationship to nature, Mr. K. said: "Now and then I would like to see a couple of trees when I step out of the house. Particularly because, thanks to their different appearance, according to the time of day and the season, they attain such a special degree of reality. Also, in the cities, in the course of time, we become confused because we always see only commodities, houses and railways, which would be empty and pointless if they were uninhabited and unused. In our peculiar social order, after all, human beings, too, are counted among such commodities, and so, at least to me, since I am not a joiner, there is something reassuringly self-sufficient about trees, something that is indifferent to me, and I hope that, even to the joiner, there is something about them that cannot be exploited." "Why, if you want to see trees, do you not sometimes simply take a trip into the country?" he was asked. Mr. Keuner replied in astonishment: "I said, I would like to see them *when I step out of the house.*" (Mr. K. also said: "It is necessary for us to make sparing use of nature. Spending time in nature without working, one easily falls into an abnormal condition; one is struck by something like a fever.")

Convincing questions

"I have noticed," said Mr. K., "that we put many people off our teaching because we have an answer to everything. Could we not, in the interests of propaganda, draw up a list of the questions that appear to us completely unsolved?"

Reliability

Mr. K., who was in favor of orderly relations between human beings, was embroiled in struggles all his life. One day he again found himself in a disagreeable situation, which made it necessary for him to go at night to several meeting places in the city that were far apart from one another. Since he was ill, Mr. K. asked a friend if he could borrow his coat. The friend agreed, even though, as a result, he himself had to call off an appointment. Toward evening, however, Mr. K.'s position worsened to such a degree that the rendezvous were no longer of any use to him and a quite different course of action became necessary. Nevertheless, and despite the lack of time, Mr. K. was anxious to keep the appointment and punctually called for the now useless coat.

Meeting again

A man who had not seen Mr. K. for a long time greeted him with the words: "You haven't changed a bit." "Oh!" said Mr. K. and turned pale.

On the selection of brutes

When Mr. Keuner, the thinking man, heard
That the most famous criminal of the city of New York
A smuggler of alcohol and a mass-murderer
Had been shot down like a dog and
Buried without ceremony
He expressed nothing but dismay.

"How," he said, "has it come to this
That not even the criminal is sure of his life
And not even he, who is prepared to do anything
Has a measure of success?
Everyone knows that those are lost
Who are concerned for their human dignity.
But those who discard it?
Shall it be said: he who escaped the depths
Falls on the heights?
At night the righteous start from their sleep bathed in
     sweat
The softest footstep fills them with alarm
Their good conscience pursues them even in their sleep
And now I hear: the criminal, too
Can no longer sleep peacefully?
What confusion!
What times these are!
A simple bit of foul play, so I hear

Is no longer enough.
A mere murder
Will get you nowhere at all.
Two or three betrayals before lunch:
Anyone would be willing to do that.
But what good is willingness
When all that matters is ability!
Even absence of principles is not enough:
Results are what counts!

Thus even the reprobate
Slides into the grave without a stir.
As there are all too many of his kind
No one notices.
He could have had the grave a lot more cheaply
This man who was out for money at all costs!
So many murders
And such a short life!

So many crimes
And so few friends!
Had he been penniless
There could not have been fewer.

How can we not lose heart
In view of such events?
What plans can we still make?

What crimes still hatch?
It is not good if too much is demanded of us.
Seeing that," said Mr. Keuner
"We become discouraged."

Form and content

Mr. K. looked at a painting that gave certain objects a very unconventional form. He said: "When they look at the world, some artists are like many philosophers. In the effort to find a form, the content gets lost. I once worked for a gardener. He handed me a pair of shears and told me to trim a laurel tree. The tree stood in a pot and was hired out for celebrations. For that it had to have the form of a sphere. I immediately began to prune the wild shoots, but no matter how hard I tried to achieve the form of a sphere, I did not succeed for a long time. First I lopped off too much on one side, then on the other. When the tree had at last become a sphere, the sphere was very small. Disappointed, the gardener said: 'Good, that's the sphere, but where's the laurel?'"

Conversations

"We can't go on talking to each other," said Mr. K. to a man. "Why not?" asked the latter, taken aback. "In your presence I am incapable of saying anything intelligent," complained Mr. K. "But I really don't mind," the other comforted him. "That I can believe," said Mr. K. angrily, "but *I* mind."

Hospitality

When Mr. K. accepted hospitality, he left his room as he had found it, because he did not believe in people putting their stamp on their surroundings. On the contrary, he made every effort to change his own behavior in such a way that it suited his accommodation, although his plans were not allowed to suffer as a result. When Mr. K. provided hospitality, he moved at least a chair or a table from its former position to another, thus taking his guest into account. "And it's better if I decide what suits him!" he said.

If Mr. K. loved someone

"What do you do," Mr. K. was asked, "if you love someone?" "I make a sketch of the person," said Mr. K.,
"and make sure that one comes to resemble the other."
"Which? The sketch?" "No," said Mr. K., "the person."

On the disruption of "one thing at a time"

One day, when he was the guest of acquaintances whom he did not know very well, Mr. K. discovered that his hosts had already laid out the breakfast things for the next morning on a small table in the bedroom. After he had initially praised his hosts in his mind because they were eager to see him on his way, he remained preoccupied by the thought. He considers, whether he, too, would get the breakfast things ready at night before going bed. After some reflection he concludes that at certain times it would be right for him to do so. He likewise concludes that it is right that others should also concern themselves with this question for a little while.

Success

Mr. K. saw an actress walking by and said: "She's beautiful." His companion said: "She's recently become successful because she's beautiful." Mr. K. was annoyed and said: "She's beautiful because she's become successful."

Mr. K. and the cats

Mr. K. did not love cats. They did not appear to him to be friends of humankind; hence he was not their friend, either. "If we had common interests," he said, "then I would be indifferent to their hostile attitude." But Mr. K. was reluctant to chase cats from his chair. "To lay oneself down to rest is work," he said. "It should be allowed to succeed." And if cats meowed outside his door he rose from his bed, even when it was cold, and let them into the warmth. "Their calculation is simple," he said. "If they cry out, the door is opened for them. If the door is no longer opened for them, they will no longer cry out. To cry out, that's progress."

Mr. K.'s favorite animal

When Mr. K. was asked which animal he esteemed above all others, he named the elephant and justified his choice as follows: The elephant combines cunning with strength. This is not the paltry cunning that is sufficient to avoid a snare or to snatch a meal by making oneself inconspicuous but the cunning that is at the disposal of strength in order to carry out great enterprises. A broad track leads to the place where this animal has been. Yet he is good-natured, he has a sense of humor. He is a good friend, just as he is a good enemy. Very large and heavy, he is nevertheless also very fast. His trunk supplies his enormous body with even the smallest items of food, even nuts. His ears are adjustable: he hears only what he wants to hear. He also lives to a great age. He is also gregarious and not only in the company of elephants. Everywhere he is both loved and feared. A certain comic aspect even makes it possible for him to be venerated. He has a thick skin, knives snap in it; but he has a gentle disposition. He can become sad. He can become angry. He likes to dance. He dies in a thicket. He loves children and other small animals. He is gray and conspicuous only because of his bulk. He is not edible. He can work hard. He likes to drink and becomes merry. He does his bit for art: he supplies ivory.

Ancient times

In front of a "constructivist" picture by the painter Lundström, depicting some jugs, Mr. K. said: "A picture from ancient times, from a barbarous age! In those days men could probably no longer tell things apart, round things no longer appeared round, pointed things no longer pointed. The painters had to put things straight again and show their customers something definite, unambiguous, well-defined; they saw so much that was indistinct, fluid, obscure; they were so starved for incorruptibility, that they were ready to acclaim a man who wouldn't sell his fool's cap. Work was distributed among many, one can see that from this picture. Those who determined the form did not concern themselves with the purpose of the objects; no water can be poured from this jug. In those days there must have been many people who were regarded solely as commodities. That, too, the artists had to resist. A barbarous age, those ancient times!" Mr. K.'s attention was called to the fact that the picture was a contemporary one. "Yes," said Mr. K. sadly, "from ancient times."

A good answer

In court a worker was asked whether he wanted to take the lay oath or swear on the Bible. He answered: "I'm unemployed." "This was not simply absent-mindedness," said Mr. K. "By this answer he showed that he found himself in a situation where such questions, indeed perhaps the whole proceedings as such, have become meaningless."

Praise

When Mr. K. heard that he was being praised by former students, he said: "After the students have long forgotten the errors of the master, he himself still remembers them."

Two cities

Mr. K. preferred city B to city A. "In city A," he said, "they love me, but in city B they were friendly to me. In city A they made themselves useful to me, but in city B they needed me. In city A they invited me to join them at table, but in city B they invited me into the kitchen."

Good turns

As an example of the right and proper way to do friends a good turn, Mr. K. related the following story. "Three young people came to an old Arab and told him: 'Our father has died. He left us seventeen camels and stated in his will that the oldest son should get half, the second a third, and the youngest a ninth of the camels. Now we cannot agree on the division; please make the decision for us!' The Arab thought for a while and said: 'As I see it, in order to share out the camels properly, you are one short. I myself have only a single camel, but I put it at your disposal. Take it and then divide up the camels, and only bring me what is left over.' They expressed their thanks for this good office, took the camel away, and then divided up the eighteen camels, so that the oldest got half—that is, nine—the second a third—that is, six—and the youngest a ninth—that is, two camels. To their astonishment, when they had led their own camels aside there was one camel left over. This one they brought back, with renewed thanks, to their old friend."

Mr. K. called this good turn a right and proper one, because it demanded no special sacrifice.

Mr. K. in unfamiliar accommodation

Entering unfamiliar accommodation, Mr. K., before he lay down to rest, looked for the exits from the house and nothing else. In reply to a question, he answered uneasily: "It's a tiresome old habit. I am for justice; so it's good if the place in which I'm staying has more than one exit."

Mr. K. and consistency

One day Mr. K. put the following question to one of his friends: "Recently I have been friendly with a man who lives opposite me. I have no inclination to go on being friendly with him; however, I not only have no reason for being friendly with him but also no reason to stop. Now I have discovered that recently, when he bought the small house that he previously had rented, he immediately had a plum tree in front of his window, which blocked out the light, chopped down, even though the plums were only half ripe. Should I now take this as a reason to break off relations with him, at least outwardly or at least inwardly?"

A few days later Mr. K. told his friend: "I have now broken off relations with the fellow; just think, already months ago he had asked the then-owner of the house to chop down the tree that blocked out the light. The latter, however, did not want to do so, because he wanted the fruit. And now that the house has passed to my acquaintance, he really has had the tree chopped down, full of still unripe fruit! I have now broken off relations with him because of his inconsistent behavior."

The father of the thought

The following reproach was made of Mr. K.: all too often in his case the wish was father to the thought. Mr. K. replied: "There never has been a thought whose father was not a wish. But what one can argue about is: which wish? One does not have to suspect that a child might have no father at all in order to suspect that the determination of fatherhood is a difficult matter."

The administration of justice

Mr. K. often mentioned as in some degree exemplary a legal instruction in ancient China, according to which the judges in important trials were fetched from distant provinces. Thus they were harder to bribe (and did not have to be so unbribable), since the local judges watched over their unbribability—that is, people who knew the ropes in just this respect and who wished the incomers ill. Also, the judges who had been sent for did not know the customs and conditions of the district from everyday experience. Injustice often assumes the character of justice simply through frequent repetition. Everything had to be reported to the incoming judges from the beginning, as a result of which they took note of what was unusual. And finally, they were not forced to violate the virtue of objectivity for the sake of many other virtues, such as gratitude, filial love, guilelessness toward old friends, or to have the courage to make enemies in their own circle.

Socrates

After reading a book about the history of philosophy Mr. K. spoke disparagingly of the efforts of the philosophers to describe all things as fundamentally unknowable. "When the Sophists asserted that they knew a great deal without having studied anything," he said, "Socrates, the Sophist, came forward with the arrogant assertion that he knew that he knew nothing. One might have expected that he would add to his sentence: because I, too, have studied nothing. (In order to know something, we have to study.) But he does not appear to have said anything more, and perhaps the immeasurable applause that burst out after his first sentence and that has lasted more than two thousand years would have drowned out any further sentence."

The envoy

Recently I spoke to Mr. K. about the case of the envoy of a foreign power, Mr. X., who had carried out a number of missions in our country on behalf of his government and after his return, as we learned to our regret, was severely disciplined, although he had achieved great successes. "The accusation was that in order to carry out his missions, he had become far too intimate with us, his enemies," I said. "Do you believe that he could have been successful without behaving in such a way?" "Certainly not," said Mr. K. "He had to eat well in order to negotiate with his enemies; he had to flatter criminals and poke fun at his own country in order to achieve his goal." "Then he acted properly?" I asked. "Yes, of course," said Mr. K. absent-mindedly. "He acted properly." And Mr. K. wanted to take his leave of me. But I held him by the sleeve. "Then why was he received with such scorn on his return?" I cried out indignantly. "He will no doubt have got used to the good food, have continued associating with criminals, and his judgment will have become unreliable," said Mr. K. indifferently, "and so they had to discipline him." "And in your opinion it was proper for them to do so?" I asked, appalled. "Yes, of course, what else could they have done?" said Mr. K. "He was brave and it was to his merit that he undertook a deadly mission. He died while carrying it out. Should they now, instead of burying him, allow him to rot in the open air and put up with the stench?"

The natural urge to own property

When someone at a party called the urge to own property a natural one, Mr. K. told the following story about some old-established fishermen:

"On the south coast of Iceland there are fishermen who, by means of fixed buoys, have divided the ocean there into individual parcels and shared them out among themselves. They are more fiercely devoted to these fields of water than to their property. They feel attached to them, would never give them up, even if no more fish were to be found in them, and they scorn the inhabitants of the harbor towns to whom they sell their catch, since these townspeople appear to them a superficial race, alienated from nature. They say of themselves that their roots are in the water. When they catch bigger fish, they keep the latter by them in tubs, give them names, and are more devoted to them than to their property. For some time now their economic position is said to be bad; nevertheless, they firmly reject all attempts at reform, with the result that several governments that disregarded their customs have been brought down by them. Such fishermen demonstrate irrefutably the power of the urge to own property to which man is subject by nature."

If sharks were men

"If sharks were men," Mr. K. was asked by his landlady's
little girl, "would they be nicer to the little fishes?"
"Certainly," he said. "If sharks were men, they would
build enormous boxes in the ocean for the little fish,
with all kinds of food inside, both vegetable and animal. They would take care that the boxes always had
fresh water, and in general they would make all kinds
of sanitary arrangements. If, for example, a little fish
were to injure a fin, it would immediately be bandaged,
so that it would not die and be lost to the sharks before its time. So that the little fish would not become
melancholy, there would be big water festivals from
time to time; because cheerful fish taste better than
melancholy ones. There would, of course, also be
schools in the big boxes. In these schools the little
fish would learn how to swim into the sharks' jaws.
They would need to know geography, for example, so
that they could find the big sharks, who lie idly around
somewhere. The principal subject would, of course,
be the moral education of the little fish. They would
be taught that it would be the best and most beautiful
thing in the world if a little fish sacrificed itself cheer-
fully and that they all had to believe the sharks, especially when the latter said they were providing for a

beautiful future. The little fish would be taught that this future is assured only if they learned obedience. The little fish had to beware of all base, materialist, egotistical, and Marxist inclinations, and if one of their number betrayed such inclinations they had to report it to the sharks immediately. If sharks were men, they would, of course, also wage wars against one another, in order to conquer other fish boxes and other little fish. The wars would be waged by their own little fish. They would teach their little fish that there was an enormous difference between themselves and the little fish belonging to the other sharks. Little fish, they would announce, are well known to be mute, but they are silent in quite different languages and hence find it impossible to understand one another. Each little fish that, in a war, killed a couple of other little fish, enemy ones, silent in their own language, would have a little order made of seaweed pinned to it and be awarded the title of hero. If sharks were men, there would, of course, also be art. There would be beautiful pictures, in which the sharks' teeth would be portrayed in magnificent colors and their jaws as pure pleasure gardens, in which one could romp about splendidly. The theaters at the bottom of the sea would show heroic little fish swimming enthusiastically into the jaws of sharks, and the music would be so beautiful that to the accompaniment of its sounds, the orchestra leading the way, the little fish would stream dreamily into the sharks' jaws, lulled by the most agreeable thoughts. There would also be a religion, if sharks were men. It would preach that little fish only really begin to live properly in the sharks' stomachs. Furthermore, if sharks were men there would be an end to all little fish being equal, as is the case now. Some would be given important offices and be placed above the others. Those who were a little bigger would even be allowed to eat up the smaller ones. That would be altogether agreeable for the sharks, since they themselves would more often get bigger bites to eat. And the bigger little fish, occupying their posts, would ensure order among the little fish, become teachers, officers, engineers in box construction, etc. In short, if sharks were men, they would for the first time bring culture to the ocean."

Waiting

Mr. K. waited for something for a day, then for a week, and then for a month. In the end he said: "I could quite easily have waited for a month, but not for this day and for this week."

The indispensable civil servant

Mr. K. heard a civil servant, who had held his post for quite a long time, praised as being indispensable, since he was such a good civil servant. "Why is he indispensable?" asked Mr. K. in annoyance. "The department would grind to a halt without him," said his eulogists. "How can he be a good civil servant if the department would grind to a halt without him?" said Mr. K. "He's had time enough to organize his department to make himself dispensable. What is he really engaged in? I'll tell you: blackmail!"

A bearable affront

A colleague of Mr. K. was accused of adopting a hostile attitude to him. "Yes, but only behind my back," said Mr. K. in his defense.

Mr. K. drives a car

Mr. K. had learned to drive, but at first did not drive very well. "So far I've only learned to drive one car," he excused himself. "But one must be able to drive two, that is, the car in front of one's own as well. Only when one observes what the driving conditions are for the car in front and can judge the obstacles it is facing does one know how to proceed with regard to that car."

Mr. K. and poetry

After reading a volume of poetry Mr. K. said: "In ancient Rome, when candidates for public office made their appearance in the Forum, they were not allowed to wear clothes with pockets, so that they could not take any bribes. Likewise, poets should not wear coats or jackets, so that they do not have any verses up their sleeves."

The horoscope

Mr. K. asked people who had horoscopes cast to mention a date in the past to their astrologers, a day on which something especially good or bad had happened to them. The horoscope must allow the astrologer to more or less discover the secret. Mr. K. had little success with this advice, because while the believers got information from their astrologers about how unfavorable or favorable the stars had been, information that did not match the experiences of the questioners, the latter then said irritably that the stars, of course, indicated only certain possibilities and that these could well have been present on the given date. Mr. K. was very surprised and put a further question.

"It is also not clear to me," he said, "why of all creatures only men should be influenced by the heavenly constellations. These powers will surely not simply neglect animals. But what happens when a certain man is an Aquarius, for example, but has a flea which is a Taurus, and drowns in a river? The flea perhaps drowns with him, although the stars may be very favorable to it. I don't like that."

Misunderstood

Mr. K. attended a meeting and afterward told the following story: In the city of X there is a so-called harumph club, in which it was the annual custom, after partaking of an excellent dinner, to say "harumph" a couple of times. The members of the club were people who found it impossible to keep their opinions to themselves for any length of time but had been forced to learn that their statements were misunderstood. "I hear, however," said Mr. K. shaking his head, "that even this 'harumph' is misunderstood by some, because they assume it means *nothing*."

Two drivers

Mr. K., asked about the approach of two theater directors, compared them as follows: "I know a driver who has the traffic regulations at his fingertips, obeys them, and is able to use them to his own benefit. He is skillful at racing forward and then maintaining a normal speed again, going easy on the engine, and thus he makes his way carefully and boldly between the other vehicles. Another driver I know proceeds differently. Even more than in his own route he is interested in the traffic as a whole and he regards himself as a mere particle of the latter. He does not take advantage of his rights and does not make himself especially conspicuous. In spirit he is driving with the car in front of him and the car behind him, with constant pleasure in the progress of every vehicle and of the pedestrians as well."

Sense of justice

Mr. K.'s hosts had a dog, and one day the latter came sidling up with every sign of a bad conscience. "He has been up to something, talk to him sternly and sadly right away," advised Mr. K. "But I don't know what he has got up to," objected his host. "The dog can't know that," said Mr. K. urgently. "Quickly show him that you are concerned and disapproving; otherwise, his sense of justice will suffer."

On friendliness

Mr. K. valued friendship very highly. He said: "To keep someone down, even in a friendly way, not to judge someone according to his potential, to be friendly to someone only when he is friendly to oneself, to regard someone coldly when he is hot, to regard him hotly, when he is cold, that is not very friendly."

[Mr. Keuner and his niece's drawing]

Mr. Keuner looked at the drawing his little niece had made. It depicted a hen flying over a farmyard. "Tell me, why does your hen have three legs?" asked Mr. Keuner. "Hens can't fly, of course," said the little artist, "and so I needed a third leg to give it a lift."

"I'm glad I asked," said Mr. Keuner.

[On corruptibility]

Once, at a social gathering of the time, when Mr. Keuner talked about pure knowledge and mentioned that it can only be aspired to by overcoming corruptibility, there were some who asked him in passing, just what corruptibility involved. "Money," said Mr. Keuner quickly. At that there arose a great oh and ah of surprise at the gathering and heads were even shaken in indignation. This shows that something more refined had been expected. Thus a desire was revealed for the corrupted to have been bribed by something refined and intellectual—and that one did not want to accuse a bribed man of lacking in intellect.

Many, it is said, were corrupted by honors. That meant: not by money. And whereas money was taken away again from people who had been shown to have wrongly taken money, there is a desire to allow those who have just as wrongly taken honors to keep their honor.

Thus many of those who are accused of exploitation would rather try to make us believe that they took money in order to rule than admit they ruled in order to take money. But when having money means ruling, ruling is nothing that can excuse stealing money.

[Error and progress]

If one thinks only of oneself, it is impossible to believe that one commits any errors and so one gets
nowhere. That it is why it is necessary to think of the
others who will carry on the work. Only in this way
does one prevent something being completed.

[Knowledge of human nature]

Mr. Keuner had little knowledge of human nature, he said: "Knowledge of human nature is only necessary where exploitation is involved. *Thinking means making changes.* If I think of a man, then I change him; it almost seems to me that he is not at all the way he is, but rather he was like that only when I began to think about him."

[Mr. Keuner and the flood tide]

Mr. Keuner was walking through a valley when he suddenly noticed that his feet were walking through water. Then he realized that his valley was in reality an arm of the sea and that high tide was approaching. He immediately stood still in order to look round for a boat, and he remained standing as long as hoped to see a boat. But when no boat came in sight, he abandoned this hope and hoped that the water would stop rising. Only when the water reached his chin did he abandon even this hope and begin to swim. He had realized that he himself was a boat.

Mr. Keuner and the actress

Mr. Keuner had a girlfriend who was an actress and who received presents from a rich man. Consequently, her views about the rich were different from Mr. Keuner's. Mr. Keuner thought the rich were bad people, but his girlfriend thought they were not all bad. Why did she think the rich were not all bad? She did not think so because she received presents from them, but because she accepted presents from them and she believed that she was not the kind of person who would accept presents from bad people. Mr. Keuner, after he had thought about this for a long time, did not believe what she believed of herself. "Take their money!" exclaimed Mr. Keuner (turning the inevitable to account). "They did not pay for the presents, they stole them. Relieve these people of their loot, so that you can be a good actress!" "Can't I be a good actress without money?" asked his girlfriend. "No," said Mr. Keuner vehemently. "No. No. No."

[Mr. Keuner and the newspapers]

Mr. Keuner ran into Mr. Muddle, the fighter against newspapers. "I am a great opponent of newspapers," said Mr. Muddle. "I don't want any newspapers." Mr. Keuner said, "I am a greater opponent of newspapers: I want different newspapers."

"Write down for me on a piece of paper," said Mr. Keuner to Mr. Muddle, "what you demand so that newspapers can appear. Because newspapers will appear. But demand the minimum. I would prefer, for example, if you permitted corruptible men to produce them, rather than demand incorruptible men, because then I would simply bribe them to improve the newspapers. But even if you demanded incorruptible men, then we should start looking for them, and if we don't find them, then we should start making some. Write down on a piece of paper what newspapers should be like, and if we find an ant that approves of what is on the piece of paper, then we should start right away. The ant will be of greater help to us in improving newspapers than a general clamor that newspapers cannot be made better. Because a mountain is more likely to be moved by a single ant than by the rumor that it is impossible to move."

If newspapers are a means to disorder, then they are also a means to achieving order. It is precisely people like Mr. Muddle who through their dissatisfaction demonstrate the value of newspapers. Mr. Muddle thinks he is concerned with the worthlessness of today's newspapers; in reality he is concerned with their worth tomorrow.

Mr. Muddle thought highly of man and did not believe newspapers could be made better, whereas Mr. Keuner did not think very highly of man and believed newspapers could be made better. "Everything can be better," said Mr. Keuner, "except man."

On betrayal

Should one keep a promise?

Should one give a promise? Where something has to be promised, there is no order. Therefore, one should establish this order. Man cannot promise anything. What does the arm promise the head? That it will remain an arm and not turn into a foot. Because every seven years it is a different arm. If one man betrays another, are the one he betrays and the one to whom he gave a promise the same? As long as the man to whom something has been promised constantly finds himself in changed circumstances and therefore himself constantly changes in accordance with the circumstances and becomes another, how can a promise to him be kept, a promise that was given to another man? The thinking man betrays. The thinking man promises nothing, except to remain a thinking man.

Commentary

Mr. Keuner said of someone: "He is a great statesman. He does not allow what someone is to deceive him as to what he can become.

"Because people today are exploited to the detriment of the individual and therefore do not want this, one should not allow oneself to be deceived into thinking that people do not want to be exploited. The guilt of those exploiting the latter to their detriment is all the greater in that here they are abusing a very moral desire."

[On the satisfaction of interests]

The principal reason that interests need to be satisfied is that a large number of ideas cannot be thought because they run counter to the interests of the thinkers. If it is impossible to satisfy interests, it is necessary to point to them and to emphasize their dissimilarity, because only in this way can the thinking man think thoughts that are of service to the interests of others, because it is easier to think on behalf of the interests of others than without any interests at all.

The two forfeits

When the time of bloody troubles had come, which he had foreseen and which he had said would consume, obliterate, and extinguish him for a long time, they fetched the thinking man from the disorderly house.

Then he indicated what he wanted to take with him into the state of extreme diminution and inwardly feared that it might be too much, and when they had gathered it together and placed it before him, it was no more than a man could carry and no more than a man could give away. Then the thinking man heaved a sigh of relief and asked that these things be put in a sack for him, and they were principally books and papers, and they contained no more knowledge than a man could forget. He took this sack with him and, in addition, a blanket, which he chose because it was easy to keep clean. All the other things with which he had surrounded himself, he left behind and gave them away with one sentence of regret and the five sentences of consent.

This was the easy forfeit.

But he is known to have made another forfeit that was much more difficult. When he was moving from one hiding place to the next, he again spent some time in a large house. There, shortly before the bloody troubles consumed him, as he had foreseen, he gave away his blanket for a more valuable one or for many blankets, and he also gave away the sack with one sentence of regret and the five sentences of consent, just as he also forgot his wisdom, so that the obliteration was complete.

This was the more difficult forfeit.

[Signs of good living]

Mr. Keuner saw an old, beautifully worked chair some-where and bought it. He said: "I hope to have a few insights if I reflect on how a life would have to be arranged so that a chair like that would not even be remarked on or there would be nothing disgraceful or virtuous in taking pleasure in it.

"Some philosophers," said Mr. Keuner, "have posed the question of what a life would have to look like which always allowed itself to be guided in critical situations by the latest hit song. If we had a good life in our hands, we would indeed require neither great motives nor very wise advice and the whole difficult business of making choices would be at an end," said Mr. Keuner, full of respect for this question.

[About truth]

Deep, the student, came to Mr. Keuner, the thinking man, and said: "I want to know the truth."

"Which truth? The truth is well known. Do you want to know the truth about the fish trade? Or about the tax system? If, because they tell you the truth about the fish trade, you no longer pay a high price for their fish, you will never know the truth," said Mr. Keuner.

Love of whom?

It was said the actress Z. killed herself out of unhappy love. Mr. Keuner said: "She killed herself out of love of herself. At any rate, she cannot have loved X. Otherwise, she would hardly have done that to him. Love is the desire to give, not to receive, something. Love is the art of producing something with the other's talents. For that, one requires the other's respect and affection. It is always possible to obtain that. The excessive desire to be loved has very little to do with real love. There is always something suicidal about self-love."

Who knows whom?

Mr. Keuner questioned two women about their husbands.

The first gave the following information:

"I lived with him for twenty years. We slept in the same room and in the same bed. We ate our meals together. He told me about all his business deals. I got to know his parents and frequently met all his friends. I knew all his illnesses, the ones he knew about and several more besides. Of all those who know him, I am the one who knows him best."

"You know him, therefore?" asked Mr. Keuner.

"I know him."

Mr. Keuner asked a second woman about her husband. She gave the following information:

"Often he did not come here for a long time, and I never knew whether he would come here again. He has not come here for one year now. I do not know whether he will come here again. I do not know whether he comes here from well-to-do houses or from the harbor alleys. I live in a well-to-do house. Who knows whether he would come to me in a poor one? He tells me nothing, he talks to me only about *my* concerns. These he knows very well. I know what he is saying, do I know what he is saying? When he comes here he is hungry sometimes, but sometimes he has eaten his fill. But he does not always eat when he is hungry, and he does not refuse dinner when he has eaten his fill. Once, when he came here he had a wound. I bandaged it for him. Once he was carried in. Once he chased everyone out of my house. When I call him a 'dark master' he laughs and says: If something is not there, it's dark, but if it's there, it's bright. But sometimes he turns somber at being addressed like this. I do not know whether I love him. I. . . ."

"Don't say anymore," said Mr. Keuner hastily. "I can see that you know him. No human being knows another better than you know him."

[The best style]

The only thing that Mr. Keuner said about style is this: "It should be quotable. A quotation is impersonal. Which are the best sons? Those whose deeds make one forget the father!"

Mr. Keuner and the doctor

Affronted, Dr. S. said to Mr. Keuner: "I have talked about so much that was unknown. And I have not only talked, I have also been a healer."

"Are they well known now, the things you treated?" asked Mr. Keuner.

S. said: "No." "It is better," said Mr. Keuner quickly, "for the unknown to remain unknown than for the number of secrets to be increased."

[Alike better than different]

It is not that people are different that is a good thing, but that they are alike. Those who are alike get along. Those who are different get bored.

[The thinking man
and the false student]

A false student came to Mr. Keuner, the thinking man,
and told him: "In America there is a calf with five
heads. What do you say to that?" Mr. Keuner said: "I
don't say anything." The false student was pleased and
said: "The wiser you were, the more you would be able
to say about it."

The stupid man expects much. The thinking man
says little.

[On having a stance]

Wisdom is one consequence of having a stance. Since wisdom is not the goal of having a stance, it cannot persuade anyone to imitate the stance.

You will not eat the way I eat. But if you eat the way I eat, that will be of use to you.

What I mean is this: it may well be that a stance leads to deeds. But you must organize what is required so that it does indeed become the case.

I often observe, says the thinking man, that I have my father's stance. But I do not do what my father does. Why are my deeds different than his? Because what is necessary is different. But I observe that the stance endures longer than the form of action: it resists what is required.

There are some who can only do one thing so as not to lose face. Since they cannot adjust to what is required, they can easily go under. But someone who has a stance can do many things without losing face.

[What Mr. Keuner was against]

Mr. Keuner was not in favor of leave-taking, not in favor of greetings, not in favor of anniversaries, not in favor of parties, not in favor of completing a task, not in favor of beginning a new phase in one's life, not in favor of settling accounts, not in favor of revenge, not in favor of definitive judgments.

[On withstanding storms]

"As the thinking man was overtaken by a great storm, he was sitting in a big car and took up a lot of space. The first thing he did was to get out of his car. The second was to take off his jacket. The third was to lie down on the ground. Thus reduced to his smallest size he withstood the storm." Reading this, Mr. Keuner said: "It is helpful to adopt the views of others about oneself. Otherwise, one is not understood."

[Mr. Keuner's illness]

"Why are you ill?" people asked Mr. Keuner. "Because the state is not right," he replied. "That's why the way I live is not right and something is going wrong with my kidneys, my muscles, and my heart.

"When I enter cities, everything is either faster or slower than I am. I speak only to those who are speaking and listen only when everyone is listening. All the profit of my time comes from uncertainty; there is no profit in certainty, except when only one person possesses it."

Incorruptibility

To the question of how a man could be trained to be incorruptible, Mr. Keuner replied: "By giving him enough to eat." To the question of how a man can be induced to make good suggestions, Mr. Keuner replied: "By making sure that he shares in the benefits of his suggestions and that he cannot attain these advantages in any other way, that is to say, alone."

[A question of guilt]

A woman student complained about Mr. Keuner's treacherous character.

"Perhaps," he defended himself, "your beauty is too quickly noticed and too quickly forgotten. At any rate, who else but you and I must be to blame for that?" and he reminded her of what was required when driving a car.

[The role of feelings]

Mr. Keuner was in the country with his small son. One morning, he came upon him crying in a corner of the garden. He inquired as to the cause of the unhappiness, was told it, and continued his way. But when on his return the boy was still crying, Mr. Keuner called him over and said to him: "What is the point of weeping when there is such a strong wind that it is impossible to hear anything at all?" The boy hesitated, understood the logic of what had been said, and returned to his heap of sand without showing any further feelings.

About young Keuner

Someone told a story about young Keuner, how one morning he had heard him tell a girl whom he liked very much: "I dreamt of you last night. You were very sensible."

[Extravagance]

The thinking man often rebuked his girlfriend because of her extravagance. Once he discovered four pairs of shoes in her room. "I also have four different kinds of feet," she excused herself.

The thinking man laughed and asked: "So what do you do, when one pair is worn out?" At that, she realized he was not yet quite in the picture and said, "I made a mistake, I have five different kinds of feet." With that the thinking man was finally in the picture.

[Servant or master]

"Whoever does not attend to himself, ensures that others will attend to him. He is a servant or a master. A servant and a master are hardly distinguishable, except to servants and masters," said Mr. Keuner, the thinking man.

"So the man who attends to himself is on the right path?"

"Whoever attends to himself, attends to nothing. He is the servant of nothing and the master of nothing."

"So the man who does not attend to himself is on the right path?"

"Yes, if he gives no cause for others to attend to him; that is, attend to nothing and serve nothing that is not themselves, or are masters of nothing that is not themselves," said Mr. Keuner, the thinking man, laughing.

[An aristocratic stance]

Mr. Keuner said: "I, too, once adopted an aristocratic stance (you know: erect, upright, and proud, head thrown back). I was standing in rising water at the time. I adopted this stance when it rose to my chin."

[On the development
of the big cities]

There are many who believe that in future the great
cities or factories could assume ever greater, indeed
ultimately immeasurable dimensions. Some fear this
and others place their hopes in it. There is, however,
no reliable means of establishing the truth of the matter. Thus Mr. Keuner proposed, at least for as long as
one was still alive, to more or less disregard this development; that is, not to behave as if the cities and factories could get out of control. "As it develops, everything seems to reckon on eternity. Who would risk
somehow restricting the elephant, whose size leaves
that of the calf behind? And yet it only grows larger
than a calf but not larger than an elephant."

On systems

"Many errors," said Mr. K., "arise because those who are talking are not interrupted at all or not frequently enough. Thus there easily arises a deceptive whole, which since it is whole, which no one can deny, also appears to be true in its individual parts, although in fact they are only true as parts of the whole.

"Many inconveniences arise or persist because after harmful habits have been eradicated, an all-too-permanent substitute is provided to satisfy the continuing need for them, which still exists. Enjoyment itself produces the need. Let me express it in terms of a metaphor: for such people who, because they are frail, feel a need to sit a great deal, benches of snow should be erected in winter, so that in spring, when young people have become stronger and the old have died, the benches likewise disappear without any measures having to be taken."

Architecture

At a time when petit-bourgeois conceptions of art pre-
vailed in the government, G. Keuner was asked by an
architect whether he should take on a big construction contract. "The errors and compromises in our art
will remain standing for hundreds of years!" exclaimed
the desperate man. G. Keuner replied: "Not anymore.
Since the tremendous development in means of de-
struction, your buildings are no more than experi-
ments, not very binding recommendations. Visual aids
for popular debates. And as for the ugly little embel-
lishments, the little pillars, etc., put them up in such
a superfluous way that a pickax can swiftly allow the
big pure lines to come into their own. Put your trust
in our people, in rapid development!"

Apparatus and party

When, after Stalin's death, the party was preparing to launch into a period of new productivity, there were many who cried out: "We don't have a party, only an apparatus. Down with the apparatus!" G. Keuner said: "The apparatus is the bone structure of administration and of the exercise of power. For too long you have seen only a skeleton. Don't pull everything down now. When you have managed to add muscles, nerves, and organs, the skeleton will no longer be visible."

Anger and advice

Mr. Keuner said: "It is difficult to give those with whom one is angry any advice. It is, however, particularly necessary, because they are in particular need of it."

Mr. Keuner and exercises

A friend told Mr. Keuner that he was much healthier ever since he had picked all the cherries from a big tree in the garden in autumn. He had crawled to the end of the branches and the great variety of movements, the reaching out and reaching up, must have done him good.

"Did you eat the cherries?" asked Mr. Keuner. And on receiving an affirmative answer, he said: "That is the kind of physical exercise I would also permit myself."

Mr. Keuner—and Mr. Brecht; or, Etiquette in dark times

Martin Chalmers

"He who bears knowledge has only one virtue:
that he bears knowledge," said Mr. Keuner.

The fictional character of Mr. Keuner, "the thinking man," and the stories told by or about him, originated in the second half of the 1920s. A number of the theater projects that Bertolt Brecht (1898–1956) was working on at this time included a figure who comments on the motives of the other protagonists or on the action. Some of the projects were not completed, and Brecht detached a number of these brief commentary fragments from the dramatic context, reworked them so that they could stand independently, and wrote new pieces of a similar kind. These became the *Stories of Mr. Keuner*, the first eleven of which were published in 1930. Although they were now autonomous pieces of prose, they shared the (Marxist) didactic purpose that had come to shape Brecht's plays and most were cast, explicitly or implicitly, as dialogues.

Brecht continued adding to these Keuner stories. A further group appeared in 1932 (although others remained unpublished) and more were written during his years of exile from Germany from 1933. One large group, including a portion of those which had already appeared in print before 1933, made up the final section of *Kalendergeschichten* [Almanac Stories], an anthology of Brecht's poetry and prose published in East and West Germany in the late 1940s. The collection was frequently reprinted during the 1950s and after. It laid the basis for the appreciation of Brecht as a popular, modern classic German author and not only as a dramatist (and writer of *The Threepenny Opera*) and theorist of drama. The thirty-nine Keuner stories published in *Kalendergeschichten*, despite their brevity, played a considerable part in establishing this reputation. Some of the shorter, aphoristic pieces in this selection, notably "Meeting Again" [Das Wiedersehen] have entered the German language as popular sayings:

> A man who had not seen Mr. K. for a long time greeted him with the words: "You haven't changed a bit." "Oh!" said Mr. K. and turned pale.

Clearly, "Meeting Again" is not a story in the usual literary sense, nor are most of the other eighty-six pieces in the present volume. Where they often come closest to "stories" is in the colloquial sense of "tell me a story" (or a joke), because they are brief enough to be remembered and retold. They share this property with poetry, of course, although this is not their only poetic quality. Brecht presumably chose the term "stories" [*Geschichten*] because he wanted to leave open what he could do with the character of Mr. Keuner. "Stories" was simply the most flexible, least prescriptive categorization for pieces that range from the anecdotal and the aphoristic, such as "Meeting Again," to the parable.

Brevity and compression are the most immediately evident features of the Keuner stories. This helps them to be memorable. At the same time, since they are written in a very laconic, lapidary prose, brevity lends them an enigmatic quality, enhancing the dialectical puzzles with which Brecht frequently presents the reader. He intended these pieces (like much of his poetry) to be "useful" and "accessible" but he did not necessarily provide easy answers. Brecht wrote many memorable lines, but he was rarely a sloganeer. (Only in the case of some of his anti-Nazi poems and stories does the reader today feel a shortfall in Brecht's literary imagination and intellectual and political acuity—a dropping of standards governed by the need to keep on providing material for the fight against Nazism on the one hand and by the inadequacy of most analyses of the Nazi regime on the other.)

More generally, with respect to the Keuner stories, it is also the case that German literature more easily accepts a variety of short and fragmentary prose forms than does English-language literature, which tends toward relatively fixed notions of the novel, the short story, and so on. This diversity and tolerance of short forms was perhaps convenient for Brecht who, it seems, easily got bored (or cultivated boredom as a manner). As early as the mid-1920s "Brecht concludes that he can't 'sit still,' he finds writing prose hard. Poetry matters more to him and even more so the always dominant plays, for the sake of which prose is frequently put aside, even though he also time and again comes back to it." (Berg/Jeske) "Time and again comes back to it"—as with the Keuner stories. Still, Brecht, who was something of a literary scholar (the sources he drew on or adapted in his poetry ranged from the Greek and Latin classics to those of China and Japan by way of Luther's German translation of the Bible) no doubt had specific models in German literature in mind as the cycle grew larger. Forms of succinct prose designed to make a point developed in the course of the baroque era in the latter part of the seventeenth century (the novelist Grimmelshausen was an exponent, from whom Brecht took the story of *Mother Courage*). These subsequently became a feature of popular almanacs, and thus one of the few types of writing to be read by the poorer classes in the eighteenth and early nineteenth centuries. This was a "useful" literature, today most familiar from anthologies of the work of Johann Peter Hebel, which combined tales of wonder and of fateful retribution with anecdotal reflections on the honesty (or not) of judges, on honor (or the lack of it) among thieves, all of it done with an eye to memorability and (moral) instruction. It was resolutely plebeian and antiheroic and did not bow down to the established order. Brecht, therefore, was both explicitly establishing a link with a popular tradition as well as underlining his literary-political intentions when he called his first new book to be published in Germany after the war *Almanac Stories* [Kalendergeschichten].

The name "Keuner" is probably not a chance appella- tion, either. As early as 1930 and 1931, Brecht's friend, the critic and writer Walter Benjamin, gave two interpretations of the significance of the name. (Brecht himself, admit- tedly, does not appear to have made any explicit comment.)

First, in a radio talk, Benjamin saw the name as deriving from the Greek word *keunos,* meaning "the general, concerning or pertaining to everyone"; of etymologically related words, *koine* means (in ancient Greek) "everyday speech" and *koinon* refers to the political community. In short, all these terms point to what is shared or understood by people in common. Benjamin's second interpretation also involves a Greek reference. He proposes that "Keuner," which as such has no particular significance, comes from the German *keiner*—no one. ("Keuner," apparently, was a mispronunciation by one of Brecht's schoolteachers.) On the one hand, this suggests a nonspecific person, without particular qualities, no more than a dialogic-dialectical medium or mediator. Benjamin, however, also refers "no one" or "no man" to the reply that Odysseus gives the blinded one-eyed cyclops, Polyphemus, as he escapes from the giant's cave. That is to say, continues Benjamin, Keuner (as *keiner* or "no one" or "no man") in the cave of the one-eyed monster of the "class state" is both "a man of many devices" like Odysseus and, like him, is "much traveled" and "much enduring." The name Keuner, in this interpretation, is itself a ruse, a device, even camouflage for the "no man" undermining the class state from within, seemingly accommodating to force, as does Mr. Eggers in "Measures Against Power," or surviving storms by making himself small, as does the thinking man in "On Withstanding Storms."

Brecht worked on the Keuner stories for almost thirty years. They constitute a strand of commentary, even self-commentary, within his writing, parallel to and overlapping with other strands in various modes, prose or poetry. The stories draw on and address political and aesthetic issues and, not least, questions of behavior; they are a guide from the perspective of the revolutionary writer. Perhaps even a guide also composed for Brecht's own use, as one author has suggested: "It seems that [Brecht] tried to subject [his private life] to some rules of conduct. These rules are set down in the *Stories of Mr. Keuner.*" (Weideli)

Nevertheless, whatever the original material or the occasion that prompted a piece, Brecht invariably abstracts from his starting point and formulates the story in as general a way as possible—general, but also concrete. As useful to the (politically aware) reader, perhaps, as a succinct aside in a play might be to a theatergoer.

For all their brevity—many no more than a few lines, most less than half a page—and their degree of abstraction, the Keuner stories *can* also be read as mediated reflections by Brecht on his own life, as refracted fragments of an autobiography, albeit with reservations. Consider, for example, the theme of exile, which is prominent in the stories. Brecht fled Germany at the end of February 1933, narrowly escaping the wave of arrests of leftists that followed the Reichstag fire. He went first to Denmark, then to Sweden and Finland, before traveling across the Soviet Union in May and June 1941 to reach the United States, where he joined the colony of exiled German writers, directors, actors, and others in Southern California. ("On thinking about hell, I gather/My brother Shelley found it was a place/Much like the city of London. I/ Who live in Los Angeles and not in London/Find, on thinking about Hell, that it must be/Still more like Los Angeles"—so begins a poem from this time.) On his return to Europe, after being summoned before the House

Un-American Activities Committee in October 1947, Brecht went to Switzerland, before accepting an offer to set up his own theater in East Berlin, capital of the nascent German Democratic Republic. In other words, Brecht had a great deal of first-hand experience of exile and flight. These are often dealt with very directly in his poetry. Here is one example, dating from the months after Brecht had been forced to flee Denmark because of German invasion. In a sequence entitled "1940" he wrote:

Fleeing from my fellow-countrymen
I have now reached Finland. . . .
Curiously
I examine a map of the continent. High up in
Lapland
Towards the Arctic
I can still see a small door.

There are many other examples of such directness in the poetry Brecht wrote during years when emigrants were "changing countries more often than shoes," as he puts it in the great poem "To Posterity."

Exile, however, is also a literary theme, a metaphor, often for the condition of the writer or intellectual. This is especially true of a culture in which writers have already experienced physical exile and reflected on it in their work, as was the case with many German writers in the decades before and after the revolutions of 1848. (Remember Heine, for example, and his lines written in Paris: "I think of Germany in the night,/and all my sleep is put to flight./I cannot get my eyes to close,/the stream of burning teardrops flows.") Furthermore, exile is a recurring motif in the Chinese poetry and philosophy that Brecht had begun to read intensively (in translation) in the late 1920s. Walter Benjamin playfully commented on Mr. Keuner's "Chinese features"; less obliquely the critic Hans Mayer suggested that "in Chinese art and philosophy the student [i.e., Brecht] found that *unity of the pedagogic and the artistic*, which he had long aspired to."

Indeed, exile was a topic for Brecht, even before exile was forced upon him. As Walter Benjamin noted, however, "the fighter for the exploited class is an emigrant in his own land." Already in 1930 Benjamin discerned a kind of crypto-emigration implicit in Brecht's work. It could be seen, he wrote, as "the preliminary form of real [emigration]; it was also a preliminary form of illegality." In addition, it should be borne in mind that the Weimar Republic, during which Brecht made his name as a writer, lasted a mere fourteen years. Even in its best days economic and political instability was never far away, and eight of its years saw various combinations of runaway inflation, business collapse, and creeping civil war.

"The Two Forfeits," one of the Keuner stories in which the costs of political opposition and of exile are most starkly delineated—ultimately, the writer or thinker pays the price of being "obliterated" for a long time to come—appears to have been written in 1930. In this story, the thinking man, as he goes into exile, worries that he may try to take too many of his possessions with him in his new life on the run. He realizes, however, that what he has chosen amounts, after all, to "no more than a man could carry and no more than a man could give away. Then the thinking man heaved a sigh of relief and asked that these things be put in a sack for him, and they were principally books and papers, and they contained no more knowledge than a man could forget.... All the other things ... he left behind and gave them away with one sentence of regret and the five sentences of consent."

Brecht typically re-used, re-worked, and adapted topics and materials in different contexts. More than most authors he was engaged in a never-ending work-in-progress. Completeness, completion were abhorrent to him. Here is a short poem from the late 1930s that echoes the sentiment in "The Two Forfeits." Unlike some of the exile poems mentioned or quoted above, and despite the use of the personal pronoun, it approaches the theme with the impersonality of the Keuner pieces.

The Note of Needing
I know many who run from pillar to post with a
    note
On which is written everything they need.
He, to whom the note is shown, says: that's a lot.
But he who has written it says: that's the very
    least.
There is one, though, who proudly shows his note
On which there is little.

Like this poem, the Keuner stories would not "work," at least not in the same way, if they could be unambiguously reduced to autobiographical incident. Consider the aphoristic "Two Cities," for example, probably written in the late 1940s and, perhaps significantly, placed as the penultimate Keuner story in the selection published in *Kalendergeschichten:*

Mr. K. preferred city B to city A. "In city A," he said, "they love me, but in city B they were friendly to me. In city A they made themselves useful to me, but in city B they needed me. In city A they invited me to join them at table, but in city B they invited me into the kitchen."

One of Brecht's biographers (Schumacher) has suggested that this piece reflects how Brecht assessed his return to Berlin in 1949 after he had directed a play in Zürich. That may be true, but in its abstraction, it speaks, rather, of a wider problem or dilemma affecting émigré German writers and intellectuals after 1945. Where the exile should "return" to was not an easy question to answer: stay in America (or Britain), go back to Europe but not to Germany, go to a German-speaking country but not to Germany, go back to Germany but, then, which Germany, as the Cold War barriers between East and West became ever more solid? In the end, as we know, Brecht accepted an offer to establish his own theater in East Berlin. But that was no foregone conclusion, even though today, thanks to the success and influence of the company he set up, the Berliner Ensemble, he is inextricably linked to the history of East Germany. Brecht, although a Marxist since the 1920s, had, no doubt wisely, chosen not to spend his exile years in the Soviet Union. Too many of his literary and theatrical friends, collaborators, and colleagues suffered or even disappeared in the Stalinist Terror. Nevertheless, in 1949 he made the decision, as had many other intellectuals at the time, that the opportunity to contribute to the building of the "first socialist state on German soil" was a worthwhile one, that the new East Germany held the promise of a more radical break with the traditions that had made Nazism possible than did the emerging Western-backed Federal Republic—although Brecht also took the precaution of becoming an Austrian citizen. In fact, the historically and biographically most direct of the Keuner pieces were written in the 1950s and refer to the situation in East Germany and the Soviet bloc in general; for instance, "Apparatus and Party," which begins "When, after Stalin's death. . . ."

Usually, however, direct reference to or drawing a lesson from events in the news is not the method adopted by Brecht in the Keuner stories. How do they function, then? A good example of Brecht's procedure is the very first story of the present volume (and also the very first of the earliest published sequence of Keuner stories), the title of which is translated here as "What's Wise About the Wise Man Is His Stance":

> A philosophy professor came to see Mr. K. and told him about his wisdom. After a while Mr. K. said to him: "You sit uncomfortably, you talk uncomfortably, you think uncomfortably." The philosophy professor became angry and said: "I didn't want to hear anything about myself but about the substance of what I was talking about." "It has no substance," said Mr. K. "I see you walking clumsily and, as far as I can see, you're not getting anywhere. You talk obscurely, and you create no light with your talking. Seeing your stance, I'm not interested in what you're getting at."

Mr. K., the thinking man, is not the philosopher as scholar, unlike the philosophy professor, who is sketched in as the traditional type of the absent-minded professor ("walking clumsily"). The latter is so busy with his thinking that he is unable to pay attention to everyday matters, but he nevertheless makes large claims for his wisdom. This way of thinking is all too much of an effort—for the body. It produces a species of self-torment. The result is obscure formulations, which provide no enlightenment. The philosophy professor's very posture betrays the fact that he has nothing to say, because he does not concern himself with the realities around him or with the person to whom he is talking. Mr. K. does not reject the content ("substance") of the philosophy professor's discourse; rather, he suggests the discourse can only have substance once it is linked to realistic behavior and actions. "Through Keuner the story ruthlessly denies the dialogue, which the professor thought he was conducting." (Knopf) K.'s reaction suggests that the professor's discourse is not communicative or dialogic, but monologic; in short, absent-minded, even foolish, because knowledge can only arise through a communication process *between* people, *about* something.

As a final example of Brecht's method in the Keuner stories, take the already mentioned and very brief piece "Meeting Again":

> A man who had not seen Mr. K. for a long time greeted him with the words: "You haven't changed a bit." "Oh!" said Mr. K. and turned pale.

The greeting appears, is no doubt intended to be friendly, a good-natured conventional expression. Perhaps at a loss for something to say, the "man" encouragingly implies that Mr. K. has retained his youthfulness, has coped well with the problems and difficulties of life. Mr. K.'s response ("Oh!") is ambiguous, could be considered positive for the second of time before we read the final words "and turned pale." The reaction is in fact a negative one. Why does Mr. K. turn pale, why is the greeting not acceptable as a compliment? To answer that, it is necessary to reflect on what "not changing" would mean; that is to say, what not learning would mean.

"Meeting Again" is one of the earlier Keuner stories. But (in Knopf's reading) its purpose (reflection on what lack of change means) is given particular force by its position as the final text in the postwar collection *Kalendergeschichten*—which would be the first time most readers encountered Mr. Keuner. Now the greeter's words would also suggest, more specifically and concretely, that fascism, exile, and war had left no mark on Mr. K., who has returned to Germany. In other words, the polite courteous phrase conceals extreme discourtesy. What happened "in between" (1933–1945) was not so important, can be forgotten or at least put aside. It's time to return to business as usual. And it was perhaps not least this atmosphere of a return to normality (and the promise of future prosperity) in West Germany that prompted Mr. Keuner (and Mr. Brecht—or was it the other way round?) to go east as so many of his fellow Germans were deciding to go west.

References

Walter Benjamin, "Bert Brecht." Originally a radio talk given in 1930. Published in vol. II of Benjamin's *Gesammelte Schriften* (Frankfurt am Main: Suhrkamp, 1980) and in English translation by Rodney Livingstone in Walter Benjamin, *Selected Writings,* vol. II, 1927–1934 (Cambridge, Mass./London: Harvard University Press, 1999), pp. 660–667.

———. "Was ist das epische Theater (1)." Probably written in 1931, but not published until 1966; in vol. II of Benjamin's *Gesammelte Schriften.* English translation by Anya Bostock in Walter Benjamin, *Understanding Brecht* (London: Verso, 1973), pp. 1–13.

Günter Berg and Wolfgang Jeske, *Bertolt Brecht* (Stuttgart/Weimar: J.B. Metzler, 1998).

Johann Peter Hebel, *The Treasure Chest* (London: Libris, 1994).

Jan Knopf, "Geschichten vom Herrn Keuner" in *Brecht Handbuch: Lyrik, Prosa, Schriften* (Stuttgart/Weimar: J.B Metzler, 1996).

Hans Mayer, *Bertolt Brecht und die Tradition* (Pfullingen: Günther Neske, 1961).

Ernst Schuhmacher, *Leben Brechts* (Leipzig: Phillip Reclam, 1988).

W. Weideli, *The Art of Bertolt Brecht,* trans. by Daniel Russell (London: Merlin Press, 1963).

Translations

The lines from "Thinking About Hell" are translated by Nicholas Jacobs, those from "1940" by Sammy McLean; both in Bertolt Brecht, *Poems 1913–1956* (London: Methuen, 1976). The poem "The Note of Needing" is translated by Martin Chalmers and Esther Kinsky. The translation of the first verse of "Night Thoughts" by Heinrich Heine is by T.J. Reed.

Note on the edition

The present translation is based on the German paperback edition of *Geschichten vom Herrn Keuner* (Frankfurt am Main: Suhrkamp Verlag, 1971). I have slightly altered the order of the pieces in that edition to place those which Brecht wrote shortly before his death at the end of the book. Pieces left untitled by Brecht were given titles by his German editors. I have adopted these, placing them in brackets as in the German edition.

—M.C.